Frances Campbell Sparhawk

Senator Intrigue and Inspector Noseby

A Tale of Spoils

Frances Campbell Sparhawk

Senator Intrigue and Inspector Noseby
A Tale of Spoils

ISBN/EAN: 9783337023157

Printed in Europe, USA, Canada, Australia, Japan

Cover: Foto ©Andreas Hilbeck / pixelio.de

More available books at **www.hansebooks.com**

SENATOR INTRIGUE

AND

INSPECTOR NOSEBY

A TALE OF SPOILS

BY

FRANCES CAMPBELL SPARHAWK

Author of "Onoqua," "A Wedding Tangle,"
"Chronicle of Conquest," etc.

BOSTON
RED-LETTER PUBLISHING COMPANY
1895

To

ALL WHO WISH OURS TO BE A

LAND OF HONOR AND NOT OF "SPOILS,"

THIS BOOK IS DEDICATED BY

F. C. S.

INTRODUCTION.

" You are much condemn'd to have an itching palm;
  To sell and mart your offices for gold
  To undeservers,"

said the old Roman to his colleague.

Two thousand years ago the " spoils " system was a dishonor.

Yet today our land of churches and missions and all benevolences bears this stigma of " Spoils."

At least, we ought to be better financiers than to give money with one hand to Indian missions and with the other to vote into office men whose example does more to demoralize the Indians than we can build up in thrice the time. What use to say that our rulers do this, when we make the rulers? " If it were in one party alone, the evil could be easily met," we say?

It will be met now, when all honest men everywhere arm themselves with justice and law, and march against it.

Let us open our eyes to the evils that "Spoils" is marshalling on all sides of us, let us form against it, charge, and overthrow it.

Among the many faults that critics will find in this book, the author points out one. It does not tell one half enough of the mischief and disaster that follow in the wake of " Spoils."

F. C. S.

NEWTON CENTRE, MASS.

SENATOR INTRIGUE

AND

INSPECTOR NOSEBY;

A Tale of Spoils.

I.

THE wind swept along the road clouds of dust that now chased, now rose and danced on before the riders as if it were a part of the grotesque procession that was galloping and checking and wheeling, turning and returning, weaving itself in and out like the bright threads of a braid, now in view, now disappearing, now glancing out again far up or far down the road, to lose itself once more, and reappear. Flashes of yellow and blue and scarlet, long streamers of all hues danced and waved along this road, and, with the earth running level as the sea to the very horizon, stood out against the radiant sky only more vivid than themselves.

And the dark hue of the wearers as they sped by added the sombre touch that was needed to bring out the full picturesqueness of this procession.

In the distance and the haste, who could see whether grime had combined with sun to produce this hue? Who could see how soiled and worn were these streamers? Or, in the swift passage, who could see how these flashing eyes failed in the steady light that reveals the awakened mind, and how these faces lacked the lines of thought and power that come with mental growth? The human animal was wide awake and filled with the sparkle that glowed in the sky and the wine of life quaffed with every breath of the glorious air.

On three sides stretched out the plain, like the tropic ocean in a calm, and on the other rose the divide, as if it were the long swell of the coming wave.

On the slope of it, and all along the top, as if this crest were breaking into foam, the tents of the Indians shone white in the sunlight.

For it was June; and ration day in the Indian Territory.

On went the tumultuous procession, leaving far behind the rough buildings of the agency and the commissariat and the broad road that here, as elsewhere, marked the incipient Western town. Up over the divide wound the trail, and down the slope to the river which was running peacefully now within its banks stretched out so far beyond the shallow water that they stood in grotesque dis-use all through the summer heat, but could scarcely hold the swollen, turbid torrent which in the autumn rains and spring freshets roared and plunged through the yearly distending gorges. The stream many a time had swept away man and horse, but for its very danger it held over these wild natures the sway of its own wildness.

And now, as men and women, boys and girls, the greater part of them on horseback, a few in wagons, more rare upon the reservations in those days than at present, forded the placid river, some of them told with many gestures the stories of their adventures here or spoke with lower breath of those whose last, fatal adventure had been here.

Then up the further slope they went and on again along the prairie, where the trail was lost in the flower-starred grass, dipped down into the brush that grew in the hollows, and wound on to a part of the divide several miles away that, being the highest ground in the neighborhood, did duty as a hill.

Here was the stockade. The cattle to be issued had been driven here after the

rounding up of the afternoon before.
Here the Indians collected to the num-
ber of hundreds, talking, laughing, greeting their friends from a distance, and
carrying on more or less that business
dear to the human heart, whether savage
or civilized, bargaining. But under all
there was attention to the occupation of
the day as they watched for the issue to
begin.

When it came to the branding of the
cattle, a little man with hair as black as
an Indian's and a complexion nearly as
dark, moved farther away from the stockade and stood with his black brows
drawn together until they ridged themselves in a heavy line of protest above
his brilliant eyes.

But he made no comment. This cruelty was one of the lessons that Uncle
Sam was teaching his red wards. The
little man was not here to inveigh
against Government methods.

When all was ready the Indians gathered themselves to the work as if it were one of the old games of Indian torture.

The poor victims, wild with terror and agony, fleeing for life without a possibility of success, ran the dreadful gauntlet which ended for them only with the fatal shot. And more than once this came from the unerring aim of the little dark man ; more than once his determined hand struck down the drawn bow with its arrow ready in the hands of a boy to bury itself in the creature it could not kill.

" You're no shots," he cried to the Indians in a tone that made them wince.

" We not want to kill too soon," returned Accowvootz stopping to reload as he spoke.

" Do you expect a poor brute to stand torture the way the Indian braves used to ? " retorted Sayre. " What's the fun of hitting where there's no chance to hit back ? " he added with that accent of contempt which never failed to make its impression on the Indians.

Queseo, the Indian chief, took a step nearer. He drew the folds of his blanket together majestically and stood looking at Sayre. The white lines of wrinkles with which his dark face was seamed shaped themselves into a bitter smile.

" Not so in the old days," he said. " The Indian hunted his bears and wolves, the wild animals ; he took his chances then. It's the great father at Washington that coops up his hunt and sends us old cows that don't know how to run, nor to fight."

Accowvootz had dropped his gun and stood listening. Pow-watz, the medicine man, came up with a long stride, all the craft in his face flaming up in delight at this rebuke to the white man. Mannab and Antelope and Humpback stood around watching.

The little dark man gazed around him, straight into the eyes of one and another of them with an almost imperceptible hardening of nerve. Then his face suddenly relaxed; he threw back his head with a laugh. "That's so," he said; and nodded.

"Ya, ya, that's so," returned the Indians; and nodded and laughed also.

"But you wouldn't be satisfied not to shoot at something," he added. "When you're ready we'll show you something better."

"You mean about the hole in the ground?" questioned Wolf's Teeth who had drawn near and with the butt of his rifle resting on his foot, stood gazing down into the muzzle.

"Look out!" vociferated the white man. "Do you want to blow your head off? *You* won't make good beef; you're too tough."

Wolf's Teeth pulled himself up and joined in the guffaw that followed. Then he repeated his question about the hole in the ground.

"Come tomorrow and see," returned Sayre, moving off as he spoke.

" Ya, ya, we all come tomorrow," the Indians called after him as he mounted and galloped back to the agency

As he went, he carried with him the picture of a young girl whom he had singled out from many because he knew her to be gentle and teachable. She was Wolf Teeth's daughter. There she squatted with women and other girls down among the dead and dying animals. With her long knife she had begun to cut strips of the palpitating flesh from which the life had not yet ebbed away. Soon (he had seen it before), her hands would be filled with the horrid entrails and she would be devouring them like a hungry animal, as she was.

The white man recalled that there must have been a time when his race also was like this, in days so long gone by as to be forgotten. His reading had not been extensive. It did not picture to him a scene of today in which gallant gentlemen and gay ladies, habited most daintily, mounted most superbly, went bolting over hedge and ditch in a land where every hill and vale bear impress of the cultivation of centuries. It did not show him the victim of their hunt pulled down by dogs and selling his poor life with desperate courage. It did not picture to him the fairest and the gayest in all that train kneeling and with her own hands severing the brush from the still palpitating fox. It did not show her to him carrying this home in token of a victory of which she would hear her praises sung in evening hours of song and gayety in that land across the sea which holds itself the proudest and the highest in all the earth. The one woman's act was through hunger ; the other's for sheer sport. The first was only a poor savage ; the last a lady of high degree.

Is this the distinction that is worth a thousand years of civilization ?

But as Sayre knew nothing of this, he

thought only of the savagery, and longed for a better law.

And yet, today, when the better law has come, where are the appliances which can make it anything but a dead letter? The benevolence that guards the dumb creatures here stretches no arm of law out to the Indian reservations. And to the great American civilization these men and women of the same blood as the white race are a thousand years behind.

A thousand years behind a people who travel by electricity! Hopeless!

How much we have done and how much forgotten since the day when the balance trembled between English possession and French possession of this continent, and the weight of an Indian's hand in friendship turned it, — for us.

Sayre went on thoughtful. But his were the thoughts that speedily ripen into action. For, the force in the man was no galvanism of office, but vitality.

He had already been here for several years; he had made the Indian character a study. It was not strange, therefore, that he had acquired a certain ascendency over the Indians although he held no post of authority, being only the trader's clerk.

It was October, and nearly a month since Sayre had drawn up the first bucket of good water from that " hole in the ground," the growth of which the Indians had watched with such interest. Even Accowvootz, the critical, had decided that the promised water was fine. Then he looked into Sayre's face with a slow, shrewd smile.

" You say it better than firewater?" he added meaningly.

" Well, isn't it ?" asked the other.

Accowvootz pointed to the open door of the trader's store, where at the moment an officer who had come down the day before was standing at the counter

stirring the liquor in his tumbler vigorously; he had held it his first duty to
inspect the drinks which it was possible
for a white man in authority to get upon
this reservation, and the trader knew
well that the more satisfactory these
were found to be, the better would be
his report. His experiment had made
him desirous to try again. Accowvootz'
eyes narrowed, and a keen ray shot out
from them as he said,

"The white man not think that. I
think like the white man."

Upon the spot Sayre had registered a
vow which he never broke. For, from
that day no firewater passed his lips.
His Indians should not be drunkards
from his example.

But in spite of this preference for firewater in accordance with the white man's
ways, the well was freely patronized
by the Indians. It was on account of
the enforcement of a regulation of
Sayre's in regard to this well that this

October morning the Indians were holding an impromptu council. Wolf's Teeth and Wahbotz had come riding furiously into camp. They had announced that they had been to the well for water, and the white man had forbidden it to them. He had told the Indians to use the well, and now he had not only refused these two a drink, but he had driven them away. They had done nothing. They had refused to go; and he had made them go. They had ridden up to the well. Why not? But he had put a fence all around.

"And now he say, 'Get down, Indian; your horse's feet muddy the water; jump off and walk inside and drink.' We not be told how to drink," growled Wahbotz.

"He order us all the time," hissed Accowvootz. "He not white chief here; we are the head men; we teach him to do as we please."

Pow-watz drew nearer to the younger

men who had brought back news of their defeat.

"He make you go?" he asked them with an inflection that caused the group about them to look at them derisively. "He make you go away? You do always as the white man say, you children. Let the old men deal with him."

Wahbotz uttered a cry of rage. Wolf's Teeth drew himself up, and his glowing eyes and working face suggested his name. It usually took a third person to rouse him thoroughly, but he could be worked into fury, as none knew better than Pow-watz.

"I teach him better!" he cried.

Then it was that Pow-watz, his purpose accomplished, nodded at the other. "Yes, you teach him," he said, in a ferocious tone. "Brave Wolf's Teeth. I help you; the Medicine Man help; he make the white man all weak. Then you fight him."

But as the words fell into the circle

there was a pause; the Indians looked at one another.

For, they were recalling a few episodes in the life of this man since, several years before, he had come among them; not his many benefits to them; these were at the moment as thoroughly forgotten as if the beneficiaries had been white men. But Pow-watz' threat had made them remember how two of them had seen Sayre on the plain when he lay down upon the ground and ordered them to strike upon a stone upon his chest. They had obeyed in fear and trembling, desiring not to hurt him. But they had told it as a marvel that when they had actually broken the stone there he had risen up and walked around as well as ever. The tribe had decided that the white man had " medicine " on his chest.

And scores of them had seen another thing that happened one day before the well was finished. Something had gone wrong and Sayre was down in "the hole in the ground" digging away with all his might. Suddenly, a rope broke in the tackle above, and the enormous bucket heaped full of earth swung loose and went crashing down into the well with a thud that shook the ground.

Underneath it all was the white man!

The Indians crowded about the opening, some with sympathy, Queseo, Powwatz and a few others with secret exultation that this light shining into the darkest of their dark ways was stamped out forever. But they all did what they could to help the white men at work to hoist up the bucket again. They bent over to espy the jellied form of the man whom they all recognized as their friend, even if he had been too much their master.

There stood Sayre as alert as ever, and unhurt save for a scratch upon his forehead and nose. As the Indians stared at him in an amazement not un-

mixed with awe, he climbed up the well
and walked off to the doctor's to have
his wound dressed. He had not found
it necessary to explain that an uneven-
ness in the side of the well into which he
had pressed himself had saved him from
everything but a graze from the bucket
as it passed him.

" He 's all medicine but his forehead,"
the Indians had decided.

It was this that they were remember-
ing now.

It was Accowvootz who at last suggested that rifles could make strong
men weak all at once and save time.

This suggestion brought about an
animated discussion in which all Pow-
watz' skill was exerted to foment the
strife.

In the height of the tumult Queseo
made his decision.

"Come with me," he announced.
"We break through to the hole in the
ground; we get the water, and drink it,

or"—he paused and looked about him,
—"or," he went on, "we teach the
white man a lesson he never forget,—
never!" And his nod was more signifi-
cant than his words.

A shout of assent went up from many
throats.

As the men were mounting, Chekotoco, a boy of fourteen, ran up to his
father.

"Let me go, too," he pleaded. "I
want to see you teach the white man."

The chief assented.

Sayre from the window of the trader's
store saw the approaching cavalcade.

He made no mistake as to its meaning. The Indians had resented his
authority. They had taken issue with
him upon a point upon which he knew
he was right; and so did they. He had
roused the evil element against himself.
He was upon trial for his life.

"It's come, Hutchins," he said to the
trader. "It was bound to come."

And putting on his hat, he walked with steady step down to the well.

He had barely stationed himself at the gate of the enclosure when the head of the procession rode toward him in a fury that was intended to make the white man recoil from his path, or else to ride him down.

But Sayre still blocked the way. And as he stood, not only was he immovable, but his face and his whole figure hardened as if he were in a coat of mail made from his muscles of steel.

When there are two, it must be one that gives way, be it ever so little. Quesco checked the pace of his horse somewhat, even as he shouted,

"Stand back! I want water. I go inside."

His horse's nose plunged against the white man's shoulder.

Sharply, as from a blow, the creature reared upon his haunches, and the hand upon his bridle turned him across the open gate.

"You may go on; but not your horses. That is my law. You must obey it." The tone of the one man unarmed rang out in command of the twenty armed, stern above his words. And the Indians could not find that the man standing there with his eyes looking through each of them, taking note of every stalwart figure and every gun well brandished, knew how easily it all might be ended, and how in an another instant they might ride in triumphant and drink of the water of victory. And with all Pow-watz' hate, this was what he would have liked, to cow the white man, even more than to kill him.

"We shoot you!" cried Queseo.

Instantly, a dozen rifles were aimed at Sayre.

Sayre placed a hand upon each gate-post, and with unwavering eyes stood there as full of silent threat as a loaded cannon in the breach.

II

T was in this moment of indecision at the sight of decision that the trader called out, "Can I help you Sayre?"

"Yes," he called back. "Get your rifle and draw on one Indian, and at the first shot you hear, kill your man." Then he said to the Indians, from whom he had never turned his eyes, "Shoot me if you like. They will punish you; and see if they will send you a better man. But at the first shot you fire, one of you falls dead. See that man. You know him. He hits every time. Try it if you like. And there'll be one dead Indian."

There was a moment's pause,—a falling back.

Sayre, whom nothing escaped, not only saw this, he also saw victory at his very feet.

Darting down, he caught up the stout stick with which he had driven back Wolf's Teeth and Wahbotz.

In a flash it descended on Queseo.

"Off your horse, Queseo!" he cried as his blow sent the Indian to the ground. "Shame on you, the chief, to set such an example. Behave better, or you'll get more than you want. Back, Pow-watz! Wahbotz! All of you."

And with a fencer's art he plied the simple weapon until more than one Indian had retreated well out of reach.

They halted then; but no one fired. The rifle that never missed was behind.

With the weight of Sayre's cudgel added to that of his courage, Queseo sullenly remounted, wheeled slowly, and rode off.

The others followed, sullen and muttering.

Sayre stood there like an embodied avenger as they turned and watched him.

When the last had disappeared, he walked back to the store.

"Thank you, Hutchins," he said as he hung up his hat again. "You trumped that time."

"Will they try it again, do you think?" inquired Hutchins anxious for his friend, for the comradeship of these two men was strong.

Sayre laughed dryly. "They know as well as I do that they're wrong," he answered. "And they're as good as white men for knowing when they're beaten,—better, I think. But the spirit will probably show itself again in some way. Our foot will have to be well on the neck of that chief before the good that's down here will have a show-ing."

"You've about the right of it," assented the other.

After a pause Sayre went on gravely, "Folks have a notion, Hutchins, that the Lord's all sentiment. But I tell you there's times when 'the Lord is a man of war.'"

"He get it, too," muttered Wolf's Teeth with a glance at the chief, and his own back no longer stung.

"White man big chief," whispered Chekotoco to him as they rode on behind the others.

Wolf's Teeth nodded.

Several years had passed since the little, dark man had won his victory at the well. Other victories had followed. He had gained the first by sheer force of character, for as trader's clerk he had had no authority to back him.

Now, however, he had been for three years superintendent of the new school started at that time upon the reservation. At the same time Hutchins had been made agent. These appointments had been founded upon fitness, and their success was marked.

The process of carting the mountain to Mahomet must always be slow, and can never be complete. Still, the Indians were rising, they were getting to the height of a somewhat wider view; for out of the dead level of barbarism a few inspirations were lifting their heads.

Already, in the minds of some of the Indians there had awakened that discontent with their present which is the surest evidence of affinity with the Anglo-Saxon race. For the most degrading customs of the earlier days had been set aside under the rule of Hutchins and Sayre, gentle or stern as the case required, and throughout the whole tribe, with a few choice exceptions, the power of Queseo and Pow-watz was steadily waning. It was with anguish that these two and their select set had looked forward to its extinction. But even this was abating. They were so evenly governed that, in spite of themselves, they could not help being comfortable.

Wolf's Teeth especially had taken to heart the lesson at the well. It was he who one crisp December day stood smiling before the superintendent.

" Napooaz come home," he said, after his greeting. Wolf's Teeth prided himself upon his English. " You see him? He George Washington now. He have his hair cut like a white man; he wear clothes; he look fine. You cut my hair, too."

Sayre's heart bounded; for only intense conviction would make an Indian part with his scalp lock. He took upon himself with alacrity the office of barber.

"Now I have clothes," said Wolf's Teeth. "Can't be white man without clothes." And he flipped his blanket with a new disdain.

But Wolf's Teeth was a head taller than Sayre, and the man of resources hesitated.

"You here to make Indian like white man," continued the other, with keen eyes upon him.

And then Sayre had it. There were in store the suits that another tribe had refused.

Wolf's Teeth in full citizen's dress, even to a necktie, which he had asked for, gave himself a long look of satisfaction in Sayre's little mirror. Then he faced about.

"Now, you give me work," he said. "When clothes wear out, white man buy more; and white man always eat. I like white man; I work; I get new clothes; I eat."

The little, dark man looked down suddenly. For, in spite of his smile, his eyes had filled. He had worked so long and so hard, and now that the results had begun, things would go faster. Ever since the day at the well Wolf's Teeth had been a devoted friend, and many a talk had they had as to the white man's way. Now Napooaz' appearance had stirred his mind and crystallized his floating ideas into set purpose. Other converts would follow. And Sayre who had labored so faithfully for this would see the growth and help it on.

Already, the forces in him were rising to meet the new occasion and use it to the utmost, as he raised his head and answered Wolf's Teeth.

"Yes, yes," he said, "I'll tell you what you can do."

As Sayre was speaking these words, two men were standing in the lobby of the Senate at Washington. One of them had just come out from the Chamber to meet his companion here.

"You'll have to think up two places, Noseby," said the senator as they walked slowly away together. "My word is pledged. My honor is concerned. Green really did a great deal for me, and Barnes was perfectly indispensable.

They're superb henchmen, both of them, something of the bygone loyalty about them. I must reward them. Think, now. And I won't forget you when your name comes up. The crush for places is so terrific that, with those I've already hoisted in, there's not a chance out of the Indian service; lucky for us there's that. Long may it survive, the fittest spoil of all."

"Yes," returned Inspector Noseby slowly, "the reservations are pretty well tucked out of the way, and nobody cares what we do there, except the philanthropists; they look sharp after us and the Civil Service. The Civil Service!" Both men stopped to laugh. "But then, senator," the inspector went on, "we have to be mighty careful, you know; and that counts; you'll remember that?"

"And tuck it on to your salary, hey? The honorable body shall be well posted as to your valuable services, that is to say, on some of them. How's that, Noseby? Shall we give away the whole?"

"You'll use your customary discretion, senator." And again the men laughed. "There's one place," pursued the speaker, " where they're getting on rayther too fast. What do you say to an agent and a superintendent?"

" Good! Go ahead, Noseby. But look out you don't run counter to our Civil Reform."

The other chuckled. " Why, senator, they're bad men. That's the only reason we have for turning 'em out. That's Civil Reform! They don't treat poor Lo right."

" Yes, yes, that's it. There's no need of further instructions to you, Noseby."

" Not much," chuckled the other.

Senator Intrigue smiled and nodded, and passed on, leaving Noseby still chuckling.

" We'll go out into the timber, Wolf's Teeth," said Sayre ; " and you shall have a lumber camp and cut wood like the white men. But you can't stay there all alone. You'll have to go down into the camp and get some of your relations to go with you."

"My cousin Wahbotz go with me," asserted the other. " And Arreep, my uncle, he go, too."

" And there's a young man ready to do something." And Sayre pointed to a young fellow in citizen's dress coming round the corner of the school building on the piazza of which they were standing.

" Yes," returned Wolf's Teeth, " may be Chekotoco go. But he like it better round here." And as his eyes turned from following the direction in which the young man was looking, he smiled shrewdly at the white man.

Sayre glanced there also, then turned himself about, smiled and spoke.

" Ah! You there, Wasu?" he said. " Come out and speak to your father."

A sweet face, not without prettiness, disappeared from the window, and in another moment an Indian girl neatly dressed was greeting Wolf's Teeth with smiles deepening into dimples. She was nineteen, and looked the prettier for the glimpses of a modest coquetry that one caught in the scarlet ribbon with which she tied her braids and the excellent fit of her woollen gown with its band of white about her throat. Every afternoon she went to school. She was now upon her way to the recitation room. She was fairly quick at her studies, and she liked the simple reading that she could understand. In the mornings she helped Mrs. Sayre about the house, and was learning to be a good cook.

And she had come to like her meat well done. Sayre's heart swelled as he looked at her and recalled that day when

he had seen her on the field at the beef
issue. He did not wonder that Chekotoco, lately returned from a training
school to which he had gone through
Sayre's persuasions, looked with more
than approval at Wasu. And he did not
object to it. If things went on as he
hoped, his wife and he would give Wasu
a pretty wedding. And then he had
plans for the two young people which
would give them a fair chance in life, a
chance that they, fettered by the past
and unassured of the future, would never
win for themselves.

And then, there was Wolf's Teeth
whom Sayre stood watching go his way
to bring more to travel the white man's
road.

"Work!" he said to himself, as the
Indian disappeared in the distance.
And more plainly than ever did he per-
ceive that work is the first of all inspirations to good, is that path which God
has appointed out of Paradise up to

Heaven, stony and steep, it is true, but with healthful air and wholesome fruits.

As he watched these Indians' first steps in this path, there came to him, strange as it may seem, something of the same interest with which a parent watches the first steps of his child. He stood there on the piazza a moment alone, planning and smiling. His face shone with delight.

He went in and told his wife. "It will all come in time, Mary," he said. "It takes only time and sticking to it."

His eyes were holden, and he had no glimpse of the sword of Damocles suspended over his head.

It was a week after this that Wolf's Teeth made the centre of an animated group, to whom he was telling his experiences.

"Wahbotz and Arreep and I," he said, "we go to work like the white man. Mr. Sayre go with us to show us how. We go up into the woods to our camp. I ask, 'We take our squaws?' The white man shake his head. 'No, no,' he say, 'that not the way the white men do, they go up by themselves.' So, we go on. By and by Wahbotz ask, 'Who'll put up our lodge for us?' The white man turn around to him. 'I put up the lodge,' he say. 'You don't need your squaws for that.' The white man know everything. So, we go on. Then we come to a place. White man say, 'This is good; we will stop here.' Indian look around him. White man is right; water near; ground good, plenty of wood, big trees to chop. Here we make camp. And now the white man put up lodge. White man do everything."

Here a reminiscence stirred Wolf's Teeth's soul with laughter and rippled over the faces of his companions.

"White man try and try," he went on. "He try again as he tell us; and he not know how. He give it up, and laugh, and say, ' Go back, Wolf's Teeth, and get your squaw, and she will put up the lodge for us, and she will cook for us.' And so I go back. But white man not lose his chance; he tell us we see how useful our squaws are and how we ought to be good to them." And Wolf's Teeth's amusement was echoed by the red men who are keen for a joke and only stolidly grave to assert their dignity to the white man. " The white man laugh, too," he said. " And he show us how to measure wood ; how to cut it. He leave us there. We begin three Indians, all like the white man. When we end, we twenty. We all get our pay ; the Indians that not work, they all stand round then, and they wish that money was going into their hands. We like white man's ways ; we like his money best of all."

And Wolf's Teeth went on to tell the astonishing fact that he had bought a pair of mules on his promise to pay, his simple word which Sayre had endorsed and which the Indian afterward scrupulously fulfilled, and that henceforth he was going to work and be rich, like the white man.

But Sayre rejoiced in his triumph, for before the end of the week twenty Indians had joined their pioneers in the lumber camp, and he had witnessed their filing in clothed in citizen's dress to be paid for their work, and he had seen the stir that it made among the other Indians, and their appreciation of the results, if not of the work. Had Sayre known of the amusement which his mistake had caused Wolf's Teeth and his companions, he would have laughed with them. For, his dignity was as real as gravitation, and as impossible to upset.

It was a beautiful evening in late April. The Indian parents and friends had come to see the pupils of the school. Wasu sat with Chekotoco at one of the windows of the assembly room. They had been talking earnestly for some time.

"My father is not like yours," said the young man. "Wolf's Teeth is a real white man. He's making money with his mules; he's a jolly teamster; he works hard. You'll be rich, Wasu. I don't like that. Then, perhaps you won't care about me."

Wasu gave him a sideways glance. She had more serious doubts than she liked to own as to the depth of her lover's civilization. He was Queseo's son, and Queseo went right because he had to do it. If the white men did not know this, the Indians did.

"My father not very rich yet," she answered. "You know how it was this spring. But why don't you get rich, too?" she asked.

"How?" questioned Chekotoco with an interest that was genuine.

"O, I can't tell you," answered the girl. "Ask Mr. Sayre; he tell you all about it; he know everything."

There was a moment's silence which Wasu broke by a running comment upon some of the visitors. "Humpback is half white man," she said. "Look at his hat and boots. But he hold on to his blanket. His daughter, she go to school, you know, and she try to make them clean up when she go home; but"—

But Chekotoco who had not answered her at all, here broke out with, "If I do get to be a rich man, Wasu, and have a good house, will you come and live in it with me?"

"Hush!" said the girl seeing that the young man's tone had made others look at them.

"Will you?" he persisted with his face still nearer hers; perhaps to speak more softly, as she desired.

The young girl answered him not a

word, but her dark eyes looked into his, until, as they dropped, his whole face beamed with smiles.

" I'll do it, Wasu," he said. I'll ask Mr. Sayre to-morrow. Nobody'll work harder than I shall. I'll hurry up, too. You'll be ready when I am?"

" I'll learn to cook well first," returned the girl, using the first excuse that offered itself to her for maidenly delay.

" What for?" questioned the other.

She laughed. " Don't you like a good dinner, Chekotoco, like what you used to have at school?"

" Yes. But I like you better."

She laughed again. " Wait awhile, and perhaps you get both," she said softly.

And if in the twilight dimness their hands met, and when she went to the door with him to say good night, their lips, what would a white girl have done differently? Mr. Sayre who saw many things which he did not look at found in it nothing amiss and was quite ready for the coming interview with one of the brightest and most difficult young men upon the reservation, Chekotoco.

For, the son of the chief inherited some of his father's qualities, pride and indolence among them, and his whole character was wavering between the good and the evil. To turn the scale to the good Sayre trusted much to the aid of the gentle girl whom the young man was seeking as his wife. With her upon his side, the white man felt himself strong.

As he watched them now, he repeated to himself, "Time and sticking to it." And already, he saw wider results in the future. He had plans for many Indians, and these varied according to their abilities. For Samoso whose white name was Will Rawson, the boy who had gone away to school when Chekotoco did and had returned at the same time, the place was here; he would never be more than a farmer and would achieve success if he attained to this. But for Chekotoco there must be a different fate; he had a clear head and a fluent tongue and at his best moments a worthy ambition. Once away from the tribe in a home of his own with Wasu's influence added to Hutchins' and the superintendent's, this wavering ambition might be steadied and he might go out into the world and earn a good living and make himself a fair reputation, as well as becoming a shining example of the use of educating Indians. With Chekotoco it was not a question of "could be," but of "would be." Already Sayre had made mention of him to his friends and the friends of the cause who were ready to open a place for him. For Sayre felt that with his personal force and the influences which he could command, he should be successful.

There were others also, one boy an artist born, Sayre was sure. He would need encouragement to push out among people of a race whose doubt of his own he had so often been made to feel ; but with this he would do well. There were girls, too, whose worth his wife knew best about and whom she meant to save from the terrible life before them.

Hutchins had his favorites as well. These three, with Mrs. Hutchins, and the missionary and his wife, often talked things over together. For upon this reservation authority, knowledge and gospel had united their strength in a threefold effort, by which, as on a cable, the wrecked lives of these young people, and in some cases of the older ones, were being run in from the breakers.

But that very evening while Sayre's head was full of plans and his heart of hope, there came on and on splashing through the mud the feet of the horses bringing the man in whose hand was the word to cut two strong strands of this triple cord of safety to the ship-wrecked.

In the churches all over the land dimes and dollars are dropping into the home mission boxes, and from every pulpit prayers are offered up for the blessing of the work among our heathen.

But the Indian reservations are well out of sight, — or they would not exist for a day longer, — civil service in Indian affairs, as in others, is our Sabbath prayer which our weekday votes have not vitalized.

And so, on splashed the horses' feet along the muddy road until they came to the end of the journey, and Sayre looking up as he heard bustle at the door, stood face to face with Inspector Noseby.

III.

SOME presences make themselves immediately felt in a room. Inspector Noseby's was one of these. The effect was as if the wheels of a machine running on time slackened a little.

The Indians looked at his open, jovial face, fair and flushed, and read there the license that gave to their laugh that touch of lawlessness which it had not needed for mirth; none knew better than Sayre how to make them gay and happy without the aftertaste of riot. Now they looked at one another and exchanged smiles; not all of them, however, for although Minnie, one of the older girls, fingered her bow with a new coquetry as he nodded to her, Ruth, the prettiest girl in the school, edged close to Mrs. Sayre as he approached and answered his affable inquiries not at all, but stood with downcast eyes and nervous fingers running gathers in her apron. The inspector with a keen glance remarked that that girl wasn't advanced with her English; and the superintendent's wife did not undeceive him, if he were deceived, but answered the comment by opening another subject.

He seemed to get on admirably, however, with Miss Linckley, the new teacher sent to the reservation a few months before; they had a good half hour's chat together and he returned the excellent points she gave him by compliments not less welcome.

But of all the people whom he met that evening he enjoyed Pow-watz the best. The last thing that he said to himself that night was his chuckle, " I must have a talk on Indian affairs with that Indian.

It was early the next morning that Noseby marched into the superintendent's office with a great bundle of papers under his arm. He had just been to the agent's upon the same errand.

"A little more work for you, Sayre," he began after a half contemptuous greeting. "We're going to have things mighty ship-shape in the Washington office; we've got to know more about these out-of-the-way places; haven't had evidence enough lately of what's going on."

"What are you down here for, if not to find out what's going on?" retorted Sayre rising and facing the other. Size and authority were both on one side, but it needed not the little, dark man's haughty indignation to prove which was the more formidable in open fight. "You want evidence, you say?" Sayre went on as the eyes of the other wavered before his gaze. "Look about you, and find it. Hutchins and I'd be proud to have you. But how can I attend to these papers this morning when my boys are just going to begin a new piece of work, and I've got to go with 'em and start 'em?"

"That's the farmer's business," retorted Noseby.

"Not for my school boys," answered the other with the suspicion of a smile that Noseby gave him full credit for. "And, besides, he's twenty miles away attending to his other business, which is enough for three men. Of course, I'll do the things; I must; but I must choose my time for it and get it in when it won't interfere with what I'm here for, to teach the Indians civilization."

Then his eyes fell upon the group seen from the window. For there stood upon the piazza of the building a dozen stalwart young Indians, Chekotoco among them, talking and laughing as they waited for their day's task to be set them. And as he looked, that loving pride in his work which is always a worker's highest incentive and his best reward filled his heart, until the frown left his face and pleasure glowed there instead.

"Every one of these fellows is reclaimed from the blanket," he went on, his need of sympathy making him for the moment forget his dislike of his listener. "I tell my wife it needs just time and sticking to it. But, Noseby, 'twill take a sight more of the results of civilization than we 've got down here to make the Indians convinced it's a good thing. They're a pretty shrewd set of fellows. That newspaper story that's been going the rounds sizes 'em well. One of these Indian fellows, I forget from where, was being taken the rounds of Washington, and somebody asked him if they would build him a house, if he would live in it? He waved his hand at one of the finest, and answered, "If you build me one like that, I will!' Ambition's buried pretty deep, but give the young ones a little of of the sunshine of civilization, and 'twill spring up, there's no doubt of it."

It was here that Noseby vowed his deepest that they should never have any of this sunshine.

As Sayre turned back from the window, Nosby was pointing to the pile of papers, Government work for him. "These are to be done immediately," was the inspector's only answer to Sayre's enthusiasm.

"Are those the orders?"

"Yes, they're your orders, sir. And I'm here to see that you obey them."

Sayre's eyes flashed. "That's not necessary," he answered. "I'll tell the boys." He went out, and after a word with the leader, returned to his office.

Noseby stood silent while the other opened his budget, supplied himself with paper, and after glancing over the first list of questions, took up his pen and began to write.

"I s'pose the poor Lo's weren't sorry for a holiday," the inspector broke out with a laugh as he watched the Indian boys walking off into the distance.

"What holiday?" questioned Sayre turning upon him sharply. "If you mean my boys, they've gone to work by themselves, to do the best they can; and they will do it. That's better than lounging, by a long chalk. We don't have a great deal of that round here, Mr. Noseby."

"Um!" was that gentleman's sole response.

Sayre wrote on without lifting his head, until at the inspector's demand he gave orders for a wagon and a driver to take him to the camps.

After Noseby had gone out Mrs. Sayre came into the office.

"Mr. Hutchins is as hard at it as you," she said. "Wasu's been up there on errand for me, and she told me."

Her husband looked up contemptuously. "All to get us out of the way, to let him carry on his investigations," he answered. "They might have trusted us. But let him investigate to his heart's content. Hutchins and I will only be the better off the more of it he does."

"He's talking with Wolf's Teeth now," announced Mrs. Sayre, standing at the window.

"Oh, is he? Well, Mary, he couldn't get hold of a better man for us, could he?" And the superintendent laughed.

And perhaps it was for this very reason, because the inspector had begun his investigations with Wolf's Teeth, that Mrs. Sayre went back to her work with a smile upon her face and her husband returned to his writing with a softened remembrance of the irritation that the visitor's presence had aroused.

Meanwhile, Noseby was interviewing Wolf's Teeth with so much interest that the horses ordered for his excursion stood stamping at the door for a good half hour while the inspector lolled on the grass in the shadow of the storehouse a dozen rods away and listened to the Indian, with a question thrown in now and then for which he took from his lips the cigar at which he was puffing vigorously. It was an excellent one and very fragrant in the nostrils of Wolf's Teeth whom Sayre had at last succeeded in convincing that cigarettes were "no good" for the health and very bad for the pocket.

Noseby narrowed his eyes as he listened to the Indian's story, and at last took out his notebook and jotted down a a few comments. "I'll tell the great father at Washington what you say about him," he explained in answer to the Indian's glance of suspicion.

Wolf's Teeth was well satisfied to have

his account of the little dark man go forth to the authorities; for they could reward him as he ought to be rewarded. He nodded, grunted, and went on.

"He like my own brother to me," he said;" he *mean* white man and red man all the same. I be dead man if not for him."

"Tell me all about it," urged Noseby poising his cigar between his fingers and replacing it. "But have a cigar, won't you?" he added; and taking out his case, held it to his companion. "Try one," he repeated.

The Indian hesitated. "Mr. Sayre tell me not to smoke," he returned. And he gave his reasons.

The other laughed. "But cigarettes are different," he said. "And they're not so bad, after all. Lots of white people smoke 'em. I do myself sometimes."

"So?" returned the Indian in a tone of surprise and satisfaction.

Noseby laughed again.

"And then, this won't make you poorer, because I pay for it," he went on. "You'll be so much in. Understand me?"

And the fair, flushed, smiling face of the representative of civilization and the dark, questioning face of the representative of barbarism outreaching toward civilization looked into each other. The inspector was a younger man than the Indian, he could not have been forty, but the knowledge of men and affairs which shone out from his eyes into those of his questioner was an *ignis fatuus* which lighted up the way of temptation as if it were the very short cut into the white man's road.

The Indian, still hesitating, gazed, smiled, laughed, stretched out his hand.

His fingers closed over the coveted weed.

Noseby smiling with a dark exultation, furnished him with a light. The

Indian took a few puffs at the cigar with intense enjoyment.

And then the result of months of labor had gone up in a whiff of smoke.

"Ya," he resumed, "Mr. Sayre treat me like his own brother. I have mules; I do carting; I get money. Last winter the roads too bad, no teams go then. Mr. Sayre say, 'I give you work like white man, Wolf's Teeth. You saw wood, you split it, you make great pile right where I tell you; I pay you; that give you money.' So, I work. I made like white man; I like money."

"But one day such a pain. A nail run up into this foot. I go home. I go to bed. Pow-watz, our medicine man, he come; he enchant the place. Then Mr. Sayre he find out. He say enchantment not enough. Mr. Sayre know everything. So, the doctor put on something good; pull the pain right out."

"Then Pow-watz come back. He

say to me, 'Bad Indian! It not white doctor, it my enchantment pull out the pain. Take off that stuff.' And he take off the stuff. It hurt more. But Pow-watz say that because I disobey him, that make it hurt. Next day the doctor come. He so mad. He put on new stuff, and he order me, 'Let it alone.' And he give me medicine. He say, 'Now you sleep, you feel better. Mind me.' I feel better; I sleep; I mind him."

Here Wolf's Teeth closed his eyes with an air of satisfaction as if recalling his interval of rest. Then looking at Noseby, he went on with his story.

"Then Pow-watz, he come," he said, "and heap Indians with him. He say, '*I* make you sleep; that medicine not do it; that no good!' And Wasu come to see me,—she my little daughter lives with Mrs. Sayre and goes to school; she try to keep the medicine. Pow-watz and the other Indians, they get it from

her; they frighten her; they throw it
away. They take the stuff off my foot
again and they make their magic to
make me well. Then they go away and
say I get well."

"But my eyes open all the way, and
my foot so bad, it all purple up to here."
And he touched his leg above the knee.
"The doctor so angry he never come
any more. He say, 'What use?' Pow-
watz say I not trust to him, that's the
reason I get worse. The doctor say I
die 'cause I'm a fool. And that so."
And Wolf's Teeth laughed softly.
"And Wasu she cry and cry," he went
on, "and her mother can't comfort her.
She run home to Mrs. Sayre. And Mr.
Sayre he come with a big wagon, and he
get two Indians to lift me in, and he
drive me up to his own house, and he
put me on the bed in his good room,
and he say, 'You stay there, Wolf's
Teeth, till you get well.'"

"And the doctor never come, and Mr.

Sayre he would n't let Pow-watz come in, not a single Indian come in, and every day he wash my foot himself and put on something. And so, here's the dead man," finished Wolf's Teeth with the laugh of health. "And Mr. Sayre, he a brother; he take up sick Indians by the roadside. That's the kind of white man Indians like."

"Yes," answered the inspector throwing away his cigar stump and rising. "Some Indians, not Pow-watz," he added between his teeth. He thrust back his notebook into his pocket. He had obtained many other data also from Wolf's Teeth, sketches of Sayre from his first coming and the full history of the encounter at the well. "I must be going," he said. "You 're good company, Wolf's Teeth. Come and see me again. And you 'd better take two or three more cigars; they're fine ones."

"Yes, they fine ones," returned the Indian pocketing them with alacrity.

At last the horses were off for the camps. But first Noseby had strolled into the office, and found the superintendent as busy as could be desired and looking somewhat harassed at the unprecedented demand for statistics.

"Amusing creature, that Wolf's Teeth," remarked the inspector.

"Yes," returned the other without looking up.

"Swears by you, you know," continued the inspector. "Say, now, Sayre, that's a pretty good put-up job, that brotherly devotion dodge. Had the fellow around here handy to be interviewed, hey? Well, I've done it; so, be satisfied, 'n' try a little less sentiment next time."

Sayre sprang to his feet. His hands clenched themselves so that the muscles stood out like cords; the great vein in his forehead throbbed as if it would burst. Noseby eyed him uneasily, and drew back a step. It was the last time

that he jeered openly at him; whatever
his purpose, during the remainder of his
stay he kept his sarcasm to himself or
vented it upon another object than this
man with the stature of a pigmy and
pluck enough for a general.

"O, you don't take to chaff, Sayre,"
he volunteered hastily. "'Twas a fine
thing to do, of course."

"I don't want praise," retorted the
other, "and you're welcome to blame
whatever you see amiss. But don't let
me hear any more about 'put-up jobs.'
We don't have 'em round here."

Noseby's laugh as he went out lacked
a little of its usual fluency; but to atone
for this, the fire in his eyes was more
than usually smouldering and dangerous, and until he drew up at the Indian
camps he in no way resembled the jovial
fellow whose expansive good humor had
overflowed upon all, with one exception,
ever since his arrival. At sight of these
camps, however, his spirits revived, and

if there was an added sparkle in his eyes as he sprang down from the wagon, it came from the triumph of finding here what he wanted.

Here was a nest of tents, and their owners were all abroad in the sunny weather. The women and girls looked shyly at the stranger, not daring to lift their downcast heads.

And yet he was not out of hearing before in their own tongue they were commenting upon every peculiarity of face and dress and manner. They contrasted his fairness with the color of the little, dark man, and decided that this stranger was more of a white man than the other.

But Noseby had little thought for their comments as he saw before him somewhat apart a group of men whom he had wanted to meet. Queseo and Pow-watz left these to greet him. They were about to hold a council, they said. Would the white messenger of the great father at Washington join them? They were trying to see what was best for their people. Surely, he in his wisdom would know. And as one and another strolled up, Pow-watz introduced his friends.

Noseby with beaming gravity shook hands all around and took his place between Queseo and Pow-watz as if it were the one thing in the world that he enjoyed most. Possibly, under the circumstances it was. For he realized how much this council was due to the few words that had passed between himself and the medicine man the evening before.

IV.

OW-WATZ turned to him with a satisfaction that shone through all his dignity.

On the way home from the school the previous evening he had turned to Queseo as they drove on.

"White man just come from the father at Washington quite different from the little chief with the big heart, Queseo," he had begun. And Queseo upon whom Noseby had also beamed, had assented warmly. "He talks well, he's a great man," Pow-watz had resumed. "It's not his way to tell us what we have to do, like the other one. He asks us how we do; if we are well;

if we are happy. I tell him the Great Spirit gives us all some sorrow. Then he says he's come to make us happy; he's glad to see us so well. I say the little white chief with the big heart make us all well; he's medicine man and everything; he knows everything; he does everything; he orders us all, we all mind what he says. I say this to him, Queseo, because I think all white men the same, he'll like it."

"That's so," responded the chief with assurance.

But Pow-watz shook his head and his voice took on a new impressiveness. "I said that to him," he resumed, "and he came close up to me, Queseo, and he looked at me one minute in my eyes, and he never spoke one word; his eyes, they talk. He going to speak. Then he turn his head. The little chief with the big heart just behind him, not looking yet. Then the white man said to me, 'Tell me all about it, Pow-watz.

The father at Washington must know everything.' Then he looked over his shoulder another time. The little chief almost there. Then he said quick down in his throat, 'It's time you speak, you and the others.' Queseo, when I hear that, I'm medicine man once more as in the old time!'"

"Good news, Pow-watz, fine news," cried his listener.

"Then," Pow-watz went on, "the little chief came up, and the white man was laughing at me. "You learn English better, Pow-watz, he was saying to me; I can't understand you.' And he kept on looking at me, and he smiled and smiled, and the little white chief was seeing us smile, — he sees everything, — he looked straight through me, I think he would drag out the words the white man said. But when he turned to the white man, he's not looking; he's gone off, he laughs with somebody else. I learn that way, too, Queseo. That's the white man's way. And I'll be better Indian medicine man."

Surely, Pow-watz was in no danger of improving his English, if he habitually talked in the fluent Indian he was using now.

"I don't know what it means," Queseo had returned.

And Pow-watz with the voice of an oracle had declared that it meant that white men were like Indians and did not all think alike, and, further, that it meant that the big white man didn't like the little white chief. "Then, what does it matter if he have big heart?" he pursued. "The white man have bigger. He ask us to tell him everything, Queseo. We tell him."

And Pow-watz' chuckle had singularly resembled the one with which Noseby himself had gone to sleep that night.

So, it had come about that the council was ready for the inspector when he arrived, and would have been ready had he come at any day or hour, it being perfectly able to hold over until such time as it was needed.

But Pow-watz had not been medicine man and Queseo chief, any more than Noseby had been politician, all these years for nothing; the tactics were identical. There was not a good Indian upon the reservation who did not hold the agent and the little chief with the big heart in honor, and there were some honest Indians in this council; it not only would have been impossible for Pow-watz to keep them out without creating suspicion, but, being unquestionably the respectable part of the community, they gave the council a flavor of respectability which was not lost upon Pow-watz any more than if he had been white. And if these Indians believed in the white man, did they not also believe in himself and in Queseo?

They should continue to do so.

The council opened by a florid speech

from Queseo reported to Noseby through the interpreter. The chief's English was good enough to be intelligible, but he would by no means have allowed himself such diminution of his dignity as to utter an English word when the great father was paying somebody to utter it for him.

The white man responded by assurances of his regard, his power and his desire to make the Indians as happy as possible, and in especial, his readiness to listen attentively to all that related to them and their affairs. He was here to find out how matters were going on between them and the white men, he had come to hear and to judge; he had the power to decide and the will to make them happy; all things seemed so good, he hoped that under it they had no cause for complaint; but if so, let them tell him fully everything."

" Ya, it all good. The little chief with the big heart, he make us work," laughed Wahbotz giving an account of their wood cutting. That's good for us; we get money; so we quite white men now."

Noseby nodded.

Story after story came to him illustrating the labors of these civilizers of the Indian. He found that there had been no lack of needed sternness, but not one instance of severity, and many instances of a care that bordered upon tenderness which he was utterly unable to comprehend and looked upon as the veriest balderdash. But it was plain that the men had done wonders considering the adverse conditions that reign upon all Indian reservations.

He was no politician, however, if he could not make one fact serve his purpose as well as another.

"No more dances," explained Accowvootz. "The white man say dances bad, they break us all up."

Noseby's eyes began to dance. He

looked his man up and down with gathering merriment, then he took his cigar from his mouth and laughed aloud.

The Indians who had all been supplied from a box of cigars which the inspector had brought with him, not equal to those offered Wolf's Teeth which had been bought for his own use, but still, fair, as his experienced taste was assuring him at the moment, — looked with astonishment at the white man who laughed and laughed, and slapped his knee and laughed again in the teeth of a command of their little chief with the big heart. But if the taste of his smoke was so good, why should not the taste of his mirth be also? Half wonderingly at first, and then with relish they joined in the laugh, and awaited what was to follow.

" Did you ever ask your little white chief, as you call him, if he didn't dance himself?" asked Noseby as soon as he found his voice. " Dancing's no harm," he pursued. "Lots of white people do it, good people. Why, I do it myself. And, now I think of it, I've never seen a first-class Indian dance. Can't you get me up one?—And I'll write out a description of it for the Smithsonian, or the newspapers," he interjected, though not aloud, "and turn an honest penny on it. —Can't you now, my friends?" he repeated.

Every face lighted with sudden pleasure, and then as suddenly clouded.

"The little white chief and Mr. Hutchins, they say 'no'," returned Accowvootz.

Noseby's side glances showed him Pow-watz and Queseo waiting with intentness for his answer. An air of confidence in them struck him in contrast to the doubt of the others what it was possible for him to do in the face of this prohibition. His acumen, then, had not deceived him; it seldom did. He was not playing a losing game.

He uttered a contemptuous laugh.

"Nobody'll say 'no' when I say 'yes,'" he returned.

"That's so," cried one and another.

The two Indian leaders exchanged glances.

"Yes, that's so," echoed the inspector taking his cigar from his mouth to emphasize his statement. "Now, how soon can you have it? And, mind, I want a good, rousing one, none of your make-believes."

"We have it in three days," responded Pow-watz.

And, so, a practice which meant a return to the barbarous customs against which the agent and the superintendent had been fighting for years was reestablished. For, as well tempt a drunkard trying to reform with a glass of whiskey as a reservation Indian who has set his foot upon the white man's road with an Indian dance. It brings back old tastes, old delights with redoubled strength.

But what would this weigh against Noseby's curiosity, or his self-interest? Indeed, it was only another means of accomplishing his deeper purpose in which so many politicians were working with him, to do things by halves and so keep them along to offer convenient occupation for many a political henchman hard to dispose of otherwise, and sometimes ill-fitted for more conspicuous posts.

As they were discussing this dance, the inspector took occasion to remark in connection with it that Mr. Sayre needn't try to do more than his own work, he had plenty of that.

Pow-watz' wrinkles showed deeper and whiter than ever.

"He do medicine man's work; he do all the work," he answered with deep inflection.

And Noseby learned the other side of Wolf's Teeth's story.

He nodded sagaciously at the recital.

"That's not the way to do," he asserted to Pow-watz. He added that he could not say more now; but he assured the Indians that in future their feelings should be considered. Unquestionably, the reservations belonged to them. They had rights,—yes, indeed! He would look after these and do his best to make them happy. They must be discreet, but they might trust him.

So, the progressive Indians who were not yet progressive enough to withstand the dance when invited to it by the white man in authority and yet who believed in Sayre and Hutchins with all their hearts, and the Indian Indians who wanted nothing but the re-establishment of their old rule of barbarism and who saw here the promise and the potency of this, alike nodded their satisfaction.

The former, however, comprehended nothing of the inspector's meaning further than a taste of their old amusement. But the latter rose up from the conference with so assured a stride and eyes so full of malicious delight that they must already have tasted of their victory.

It was that very evening that Wolf's Teeth with Indian facility for gathering and distributing news learned of this council and commented upon it to the superintendent.

"Queseo and Pow-watz, they grown whole foot taller," he announced. "They going to have a war dance next week. The new white man, he order it. It must be they got some white man's scalp, somehow," he mused.

A chill ran through Sayre. He felt a hidden significance in the words. Was there to be really a white man's scalp, and that scalp his own, in the dance which the white man had instigated? Were all these investigations going on from hour to hour about things trivial to puerility, all these questions that seemed asked to perplex rather than to arrive at facts, all these demands for increased work of a nature that diverted from what he considered the real work, all these confabs with different Indians, chiefly with the disaffected ones, tending to one end?

The agent looked in that evening. Sayre put the question to him. "Hutchins," he said, "what do you think? Are they after our scalps? Is the political tomahawk heaved up for our benefit?"

"Looks mighty like it in some ways," returned the other. "The fellow's setting everything topsy turvy and undoing our best work. I shouldn't have said 'twas possible to get through so much mischief in twenty four hours. I'd like to know what it means."

There fell a silence between the two which Sayre broke by saying, "I've never had any difficulty in earning my living, and it would go hard with me if

I couldn't get a better one somewhere else. And, then, my children will have to be sent away to school soon, and it's a dog's life as to work. And yet, Hutchins, there's more than that in it. This work gets a hold on one. I s'pose in one way it's the best work that's given to a man to try to level up his fellows. But whatever the reason is, 'twould be an awful tug to pull out of it. But if somebody came who'd do it better, or as well, I'd be willing. But it doesn't look that way."

Hutchins uttered something that was meant for a laugh and turned out nearer a groan.

" Politically, Sayre, these Indians are carrion to vultures," he answered.

" And then, what would our good fellows do if Queseo and Pow-watz should be allowed to get on the top and crow ? " asked Sayre.

" Looks as if that was what they're going to do now," said the other.

"Never! Wait till that fellow clears out, and as long 's my head's on my shoulders, up to the very last minute, my foot 's on neck of Indian tyranny."

The little, dark man had sprung up in his earnestness, and one who did not know him looking into his set face and flashing eyes, would yet have been sure of his ability to make his word good. Suddenly, he turned to his friend with a smile of rare sweetness.

"You won't think I'm intending to usurp your functions, Hutchins?"

The agent laughed. "That's the last thing we shall quarrel over, Sayre, as long's the work's done," he answered. "At any rate," he added after a pause, "Noseby can't complain of our idleness."

And then these two men who were not deeply engrossed by their personal affairs passed on to the discussion of the details of their work, and, especially, of how they should cope with the spirit of disorder following in the wake of the inspector.

The inspector had finished his tour of investigation which ended soon after his visit to this reservation, when one morning he presented himself at the door of Senator Intrigue's fine residence in Washington.

"The senator's too busy to see anybody," announced his secretary. "He's preparing his great speech on 'Political Reform.'"

A broad smile overspread Noseby's countenance. "Ah! indeed," he said. "That's good. But you'll do me the kindness to take him this at once." And he handed his card.

"He gave strict orders that he would see no one," responded the other positively.

"Young man, you'll take that card to him at once," returned the visitor with a threatening air. "And be quick; it's business of importance. It's his business, not the state's, blockhead."

" O, I see, sir. Excuse me."

And the secretary disappeared, to return again almost immediately. "Walk this way if you please, sir," he said deferentially.

And he guided the inspector through the fine hall, up the stairs where they trod on velvet and past beautiful and costly pictures and carved furniture that the veriest boor would have found magnificent. The man as he went on had time to vow that the day should come when trappings like these should be his own also, and that petty obstacles, like honor and conscience, should not stand in the way. The very sight of the luxury made him tingle and gave new stimulus to his greed which had not needed this.

Then he was ushered into the presence of the senator who was in the midst of his sentence declaring that the

interests of the country which contained
sixty four million souls clad in flesh
should be paramount to every party
purpose — of the other side.

"Ah, well, Noseby, here you are.
Glad to see you. Sit down."

And Intrigue without rising laid down
his pen and waited for the secretary to
withdraw, which he did immediately and
noiselessly.

And then the senator and the inspector sat a few moments looking
steadily at each other in silence.

"Well, how have you sped?" asked
the former finally.

Noseby's fair face glowed darkly with
triumphant malice.
"Would you like to hear a few extracts
from my report before it's given in?" he
demanded.

The other nodded. The two men
smiled at each other a moment, and
Noseby drew forth his note book.

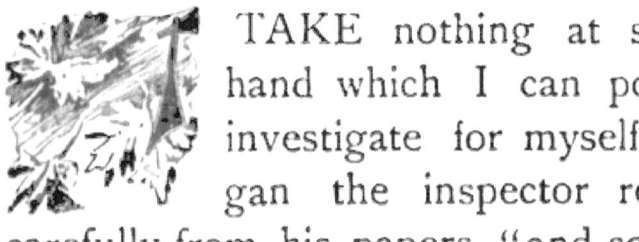 TAKE nothing at second hand which I can possibly investigate for myself," began the inspector reading carefully from his papers, "and so I can claim for my report that it is absolutely reliable. In the case of the —— reservation I found reason to suspect that matters were not quite as we could wish,'—how's that senator?" And he nodded with a smile at Intrigue who nodded back smilingly.

"The Gospel truth, Noseby."

"And so I took especial pains there," pursued the inspector. "I went down into the camps and talked with the Indians. Poor fellows, they have grievances enough. It's unpardonable there should be such utter disregard of their feelings and prejudices as I found there. What hope of civilizing them have we until we can get their good will? And how can we get it by such means as I found common there? We must move slowly in order to avoid the danger of a retrograde, always so harmful. But I found the most harmless dance forbidden; and as for cigarettes, the poor fellows had been told that these were the machinations of the devil who devised them to empty their pockets and is now lying in wait to destroy the poor wretches, body and soul, with these innocent weapons." Noseby interrupted his reading to look up and say with a face weathed in scorn, "As if even that stupid fellow, the Evil One, would want a dead Indian any more than we do a living? For my part, he might have 'em all today, but for the convenience of the present arrangement."

" De—cidedly!" echoed the senator. " But go on. That's a fine prologue."

" There's a repression and violence exercised over the whole reservation, or I should say over all the Indians who're not devoted and slavish followers of the agent and the superintendent."

"'Slavish followers'!" echoed Intrigue. " I didn't know slavishness was the Indian cut."

" Doesn't it sound well and strengthen the idea of coercion?" queried Noseby.

" To be sure."

"Then, why do you object to it?"

" My good fellow, I was only asking for my own information."

" For your information, then, it's simply the old struggle for power. Being only Indians, they're just as fond of their own way as if they were— senators."

"I see. 'Slavish' following, then, let it be."

" As a sample of the way things have

been done," pursued Noseby, "that man, Sayre, has been known to get out of his bed and go down into the camps in the middle of the night and break up a party of his Indians gambling with the Indians of a neighboring tribe. If a sharp lecture wouldn't scatter them, he'd try a whip.

The senator laughed. "Spunky fellow," isn't he?"

"But," returned the other gravely, "there's a special reason why such 'spunk' must be put a stop to. It doesn't waste itself all in such useless channels as this. I suspect strongly, though they were too clever to give me all the proof I wanted, that the people down there are in collusion with those Eastern philanthropists, as they're called, the different societies, you know, and are giving 'em points in the Indian work."

The senator's lounging attitude changed instantly.

"That'll never do," he cried. "Never, never in the world. Why, Noseby, — but go on. Let me hear your report."

"I was speaking about Sayre breaking up the gambling, wasn't I? And many a time the Indians have given him their money to keep for them, lest they should gamble it away. 'Twould take considerable witnessing, senator, and of the kind I haven't got, to convince us that that money wasn't as completely lost to the poor Lo's, and without their having had the enjoyment of spending it themselves. In short," and here the inspector searched along his page and faithfully followed copy, "I find, I say, that arbitrary measures have again and again been resorted to and that the free and natural exercise of instincts which is necessary to the enjoyment of life has in many ways been denied these Indians who, if they are passing away, should be at least allowed to pass away with kindness."

" And as speedily as possible," interpolated Intrigue.

" But in that case what would become of our friends?" questioned the inspector fastening his eyes for a moment upon the face of the senator.

" Right, Noseby, quite right. Personal predilections must not interfere with business. Go on."

" I find many examples of this spirit which I have on hand to heap up for conviction in case of need, to strengthen the dose ; but there's no need of tiring you with the whole of 'em. Here's a case in point. 'I find also in the superintendent,' " he read, " ' a flagrant act of derision and offence to their medicine man who is, really, priest and prophet of their tribe, a thing wholly unnecessary and done to curry favor with the Indians of his side, to the total disregard, I might say, injury, of all the others.' " And Noseby gave Pow-watz' version of Wolf's Teeth's story; he made no mention of anything learned in conversation with the latter; this was off the lines; decidedly, the senator would not have wanted it. "'Now, we know,'" he went on quoting carefully from his notes, "'though an incantation can do no good, it must in the nature of the case be harmless. And to take a man out from under the care of his friends and relatives in this manner was simply outrageous. I don't wonder the medicine man was excited when he told me of it, even alarmingly so. Not to let a poor fellow die among his own is a cruelty not to be condoned.'"

"And did the fellow die after all?"

Noseby laughed and nursed his knee.

"Can't catch you napping, senator," he retorted. "No, he didn't die. He's as well as you or I at this minute. But what of that? He might have died; he certainly would have died. And so, isn't the cruelty just the same? Don't go to spoiling my effects that I've worked up so hard."

" Indeed I won't," returned the other. Both men laughed.

" Hutchins and Sayre are so mixed up, you couldn't accuse one without the other," the inspector went on. " And that's lucky for us. The government has put two men down there to do the work of five, — and I've been round and picked up all the fifth don't do."

" The fifth?" questioned Intrigue.

" Yes, the fifth. They do four men's work, and more. But they're lazy on the fifth, and I'm sharp after everything they've left out on that. It's going to tell finely. 'Many important things left undone; too much laziness, anyway.' I've got dozens of things, big and little, tucked away here in my notebook; too little clerical work's one thing. You don't care to have me go through the list, I s'pose!"

" You can prove them all?" asked

Intrigue. "That's to say, Noseby, prove them in your own way, you know."

"Prove 'em!" echoed the other with the very tone of injured innocence. "What do you take me for? Do you s'pose there's the least doubt of my being able to prove everything I've got here? And you may be sure I sha'n't throw in my asides to you by way of explanation," he laughed. "No, sir!" he went on warming with his subject, "there's no doubt, not a particle,— NOT EVEN IF I HAD TO PROVE 'EM. But that's out of our line, you see. We don't prove; we STATE. In this enlightened age, senator, we don't hang a fellow on one man's testimony. BUT WE CUT OFF HIS HEAD!"

The inspector's peal of laughter was echoed by the man whom his state had sent to guard the honor of her name.

"Pretty good!" he cried. "It's the one man affair that's our tower of strength, Noseby."

The other nodded. "'Twould n't answer to have jury investigations," he returned with a laugh. " Let's hold like the grip to the one man evidence. Long may it wave!"

" Yes," returned the senator with an expression of bitter irony,

" ' long may it wave
O'er the land of the free and the home of the brave.' "

Again the inspector laughed. Then the talk drifted to desultory news from different reservations and about different people. Noseby told with infinite gusto how an agent, a friend of his, had wanted the place of superintendent on a certain reservation for a cousin of his own, and not being able to succeed in his efforts to oust the superintendent, he had succeeded in having the superintendency abolished.

"And at least that left him a good deal freer," commented the senator.

But soon he returned to the matter in hand.

"That suggestion about the danger of a jury," he began, "reminds me of what you said about the men down there being in collusion with these Eastern people, these societies. This must n't be allowed upon any account whatever. Once let this fad of co-operation get a grip on those young Indians, and our day has gone. Why, you tell me they 're trying to get them to think and act for themselves in-stead of hanging round waiting for the government to provide for them, its precious wards. But I say, let 'em hang. Precious little it will do for 'em so long as you and I and those who believe like us are to the fore. Ours is a defensive war, Noseby, we must keep off the enemy at any cost, AT ANY COST, I say. We must cut the connections."

"Rather ticklish business, is n't it?"

inquired the inspector with great interest.

"Not at all," smiled the other, "if we go at it properly. We can't switch off the men at this end of the line, nor buy them up. BUT WE OWN THE OTHER END. There's where we must make the break,—cut, or drop the other end, it's all the same. And 'twill have to come from a cut, anyway."

"A cut?"

"Yes. Don't you see, Noseby? Cut the salaries. There's the great army of the unemployed would send out volunteers for next to nothing. We should be able to buy up just such men as we want, souls and all, for much less than the salaries we pay the Sayre kind. Probably there is n't a man here,—well, to put it rather strongly,—who would n't be glad to get a friend or two in, just to get rid of him. So, that in one way or another we ought to be able to hold the field by occupying it."

They laughed, and Noseby added, "Oh, as to that, I'll warrant there wouldn't be reservations enough to go round."

"Rotation in office, that's what we want here especially," resumed Intrigue with decision. "Why, do you begin to realize what the opposite has done to us? Take these two Eastern schools. In one case Government can't put the head out,—well, for that matter, it can't in the other either. There's where the societies come in; they'd raise one infernal howl through the land. We don't dare; that's the only reason why we don't do it. But what's the consequence? A fifteen years' chance well used, — oh, it means a stride straight over the neck of our system. Where should we have been if those Western men had had such a chance? But they never shall; it's only the nearness to their friends that would give 'em a chance? Indians in the abstract nobody cares for. But these Eastern schools bring 'em too near ; they begin to grow individual,— AND THEY SHOW UP TOO WELL. Noseby, the Eastern schools must be choked off."

In his earnestness the senator leaned forward, and his voice rose to impressiveness.

"Easy to say," returned the other. "But, as you've remarked just now, it's been tried before. And then, all the commissioners take to these."

"All the commissioners don't vote the supplies. WE DO. What have you to say to this? Mind you, Noseby," he went on, "I don't recommend the wholesale way of doing things. Slide down gradually and undermine the service. As long as we can't kill off the Indian, we'll use him. I hate him," he added with emphasis.

"So do I," returned Noseby. "When you try me with that soft berth, senator,"—

" You see how all this thing works,"
the other went on without heeding him.
"Put first-class people out there, and
intercourse breeds interest here; and
interest wakes up the people. Our saf-
est, if not our richest field will be lost.
So, the economy that saves money for
the country by this cut on the salaries
works in two ways; economy is always
popular, and it keeps the Indian field in
our hands."

" There's one thing more, senator, in
regard to congressional economy that
you forgot to mention," said Noseby
bending a trifle nearer his companion
than was agreeable to the companion.
For the senator was in no way unmind-
ful of the distance that separates the
gentleman who pays for his work to be
done for him and the villain who does it
for the pay. But his sudden haughtiness did not disconcert the man who
had resolved to stand one day as high
as he, even to surroundings. " Econ-

omy in some ways," he went on, "gives a man a chance to do a fair thing for himself in another way. That's what people ought to expect. You're here to spend the Government money, you congressmen, and to choose your own way of doing it."

And leaning back in his chair, his eyes, by chance, lighted upon a choice painting that Intrigue had just bought and that, it happened, had actually come from money which the senator had known how to make his position yield him so liberally.

The other moved uneasily, eyed Noseby with a stare, which, as it produced no other effect than an indulgent smile, gave way to a look of comprehension under which he strove to hide the embarrassment that he had the grace to feel. But this, too, gave way when he perceived how completely a matter of course this use of his opportunities appeared to his companion.

With one of the inconsistencies of human nature, he scored this trait against Noseby in his future dealings with him as the mark of a dangerous unscrupulousness. But at the moment he returned the smile, and the education which, for good or ill every man bears with him for every other man was not lost upon the inspector.

"It's worth something, senator, recollect," said Noseby as he rose to go, "to turn men on true evidence,— true on one side, you know,— out of the best governed reservation in the service; and I shall have hard work to do it; for some of the powers that be actually don't object to good men."

"Well, aren't you capable of it?"

Noseby winked. The senator had to stand it; he needed him.

"Is it really the best governed reservation in the service?" he asked.

"Yes. Don't you want a good place for your friends?" They'll find things in fine order,—if I haven't tipped 'em up a bit," he added under his breath.

"Things won't stay so long, I'll be bound," returned the other, "for Green has never seen an Indian, and Barnes hates 'em as much as we do. But then, the fellows will get in, and it's not my fault if they don't stay."

"Make room for the next ones," suggested the inspector with the smile that Intrigue did not like when it was directed against himself.

"If you succeed with my men," he began, when the other interrupted him.

"It's my business to get the others out," he said, "and I'll bet on doing it. Why, the sheer goodness of their superiors will settle the whole business. I've only to present the case in my own powerful way, hey, senator? But as to putting the others in,—they've been in Government service somewhere a while ago, you say, which makes it easier. But, anyway, it's your racket, and I presume you know how to work it. If not, 'twill be the first neat little job you ever did get stuck on."

The other shrugged his shoulders. "If you succeed," he answered, "be sure I won't forget my part of the contract."

"No," returned Noseby with a laugh, "I'm quite sure you won't. It's not your way to forget your friends," he pursued ignoring the congressional frown.

"And you're confident of success?" questioned the senator with a touch of that haughtiness which would be overwhelming in case of failure.

"Confident? When I've found fault with everything from the food straight up, or down! Yes, I'll bet on that." He smiled at Intrigue. "Do you forget that before I went down I knew just what I was to find?" he asked. "We sized up the business, you recollect, and got points on the things considered the most objectionable. I have 'em all here." And he touched his note book. "You can always find what you look for, if it's fault," he went on. "And, then there was a nice little girl down there in the school to help me; she didn't mind giving me points, and plenty of 'em; and I suspect that certain things I particularly wanted would have been missing if she hadn't made 'em for me. So kind in her! I gave her no end of compliments, which she appreciated vastly. But she would like something rather more solid, you know, —promotion, for instance. I promised it to her. I hope you'll help me to get it for her. It wouldn't be bad for your friends, either. You see, scalping these fellows all in a minute early in June will give your friends a chance at next year's nominations."

"Certainly, certainly," responded Intrigue making a few hurried notes and evidently anxious to get rid of his visitor, and determined to get rid of him in another way by giving him the utmost of his desire politically, even if this were a post that he was notoriously unfitted for. "I'm all ready when the thing's done to carry out my part of the agreement," he repeated, rising and edging the other toward the door. "So, that's a sure thing.'

"That's fair play!" laughed the other. "And good morning to you, senator." And he went out smiling.

"He might have said 'Thank you,'" muttered Intrigue. "But, after all, the one thing important is to provide for my friends, and then to get rid of him." He sat down and took up his pen again.

It was some time, however, before he could collect his thoughts to go on with his work.

Noseby, still smiling, large, florid, fluent, successful and living only for success, worshipping it as the idol of

his dreams, conscious — through his
long course of ignoring them, — of
obligations to no other human being
than himself, unless to those whom he
served through self-interest, ran down
the steps of Intrigue's house, and in
his swift landing on the sidewalk almost
upset a man with whom he sharply
collided. He laughed, apologized, and
hurried on, muttering to himself, still
laughing,

" Old star-gazer ! "

It was true that the man was gazing
at the stars as, high overhead, they
floated out against the sky as deep a
blue as the azure in which these were
set. For it was Decoration Day. And
this old man's eyes were dim and the
pain filled his heart with its old keen-
ness. It seemed to him to be down-
ward that he was gazing into a grave
in which lay his only son who should
have been the staff of his old age. The
flag had been draped around him, the

flag he had died for in those days when the land teemed with heroes. This son, dead with a wound in the breast, had helped to mend the ghastly rent in the dear old flag. It had been knitted together, it seemed to the old man, with the very life tissues of those who had died for it ; the blood of their courage had reddened its stripes, the purity of their devotion made fairer its whiteness, and their loyalty had been like the deep background of its stars, that background from which the stars of our union shine out.

He seemed to see the processions winding through the graveyards of the land and laying their tributes of flowers at the graves of its soldiers. At the moment he felt life all the more lonely. But it was joy that through all the sad years past and to come, the dear old flag had waved and would wave unstained and without the loss of a star.

" Old star-gazer ! " Noseby had called him in open scorn.

For what cared Noseby and Intrigue who had fought and won the battles ? To them the question was of spoils. The dead were welcome to their empty honors, so long as they themselves held the substance.

And so, while Intrigue prepared to work his will in his own place, Noseby with the buoyant step of a triumph already won, walked on to the delivery of his official report, a report that through many true statements warped to suit his purpose, he had made to read so like the truth that an honest desire to act with fairness upon it was not likely to penetrate the disguise without the weapons of further evidence. And, even if it could, what power Noseby and his colleagues had to carry through their purpose! Everywhere were men and reinforcements for them. Resistance on all sides was impossible. And let them once make a gap and spring into it, and defence was hopeless; the fortress was won, — not betrayed, it may be, but conquered.

So, while Sayre and Hutchins were putting down again that element of insubordination to civilized rule which the presence and authority of Noseby had made rampant, the official gallows was being built for these Mordecais whose honor was a reproach to the dishonor of their superiors.

VI

AY had come, and gone; and the expectancy which had followed Noseby's visit had died out in the hearts of the Indian leaders. The vigorous rule which had asserted itself once more seemed to them not only inflexible, but permanent. With Pow-watz, to be sure, hope still lingered, and he expressed this to Queseo. But the chief was not sanguine, and the two had ceased to discuss the matter, even with the head men.

It was almost the middle of June, the late afternoon of a sultry day, that Wasu and Chekotoco sat on a rude bench under a tree in the school grounds. They were acknowledged lovers, and not only did life run for them in the "golden sands" suited to this fact, but there was in their future an actual brightness and hope. The young Indian had shown himself of better stuff than Sayre had at one time dared to dream was in him, and there seemed no reason why these two should not have as free and happy and civilized a life among the healthful influences of civilization as any young white couple.

That afternoon they had been sitting silent awhile, the young man pondering over some information that he had received, when he turned to Wasu.

"And are they all talking about us Indians?" he asked. "And do they do it often, you say?"

As he spoke, he nodded toward the window of a corner room in the school building, — Mrs. Sayre's parlor, — through which figures could be seen and from which floated out the sound of eager voices.

"Yes," answered Wasu, "they talk

about Indians, Mr. Hutchins, and Mrs. Hutchins, and the missionaries, and Mr. and Mrs. Sayre. They talk about us often, what they shall do for us. Mrs. Sayre told me."

Chekotoco's eyes wandered from the window and the school grounds far out over the plain to the horizon where the sky of June met the earth in a blue as deep as that of the summer sea, except over the divide where the warmth of coming sunset had mellowed it to the zenith. The vivid impressions of his school days had been somewhat worn away by the attritions of reservation life, and this landscape which enclosed his present looked to him large and important.

And yet the life beyond this horizon, the one like his past, had its keen attractions for him. It was the power of reaching forth to this outside life which gave the white man his importance in the Indian's eyes.

He looked down at the little figure beside him. " Perhaps they're talking about *us* now, Wasu," he said.

Wasu blushed and smiled, like any white girl whose wedding day is only a week off and who feels the whole air astir with preparations, and believes, although she will not say it, that there can be nothing so important this side of the event.

"Yes, they talk of us part of the time," she answered demurely. "They have so much to do for us. Mrs. Sayre, she take so much trouble. But she say it not too much for a good girl like me."

" That's so," returned Chekotoco, his face radiant.

And while the people in conclave in the house discussed the affairs of the reservation with that unity of interest and purpose which enabled them to do much excellent work and to make in many places beginnings which with time

and care would lead to fine results, the
lovers sat and talked of the future that
would be opened to them through this
very care and zeal. If white men and
women elsewhere were like these, the
young Indians were more than ready to
go out among them and take their
birthright. Chekotoco's ambition had
been stirred and his love for Wasu
appealed to as a stimulus to urge him
forward. And Wasu's ambition was
unflagging.

As they sat there a figure came up
to the gate and passed through, and
Wolf's Teeth strode up and sat down
beside them. He was full of the fine
wedding for his daughter that was coming off so soon.

"Big tubs lemonade," he said, "and
all the Indians have all they want. Indians all fishes that day, they so dry.
And then they have feast, too. The
white man give it. Cost heap money.
When you go out, Wasu, with the white

people, you get heap money, too. You
give us a feast. What say, Chekotoco?" And the Indian broke into a
laugh of amused anticipation.

The others laughed also, with no
dissent in their tones; and in some way
the distance and strangeness which
Wolf's Teeth had dreaded so much in
their going away, though he would not
speak of them, were lessened.

Wolf's Teeth told what he had been
doing, how Napooaz, whom he now
always called George Washington, had
settled down to farming like any white
man, how Accowvootz liked to hear the
money jingle in his pockets and for this
reason was coming to exert himself
more and more; how his uncle, Arreep,
had given up storing his things in the
house that had been built for him and
had gone into it himself to live. And
many other changes he spoke of which
had come about through the labors of

these people now in conference in Mrs. Sayre's little parlor.

At last he turned to Chekotoco. The amusement had gone from his face, and even his manner had gained the dignity of intense earnestness.

"Chekotoco," he said, "you go out among white men. You the son of our chief; you stand first here. You stand first there; you work; you make them find out Indian somebody. Will you?"

A flash in the young man's eyes answered the fire in Wolf's Teeth's. Wasu slipped her hand into her lover's, and as she met its pressure, she turned to her father.

"Yes, he will," she answered, her face lighting up with earnestness.

"Yes, I will," said Chekotoco. "They'll see the Indian is behind nobody."

The older man nodded his satisfaction. "Ya, ya," he said. "That good.

You do well; then we try some more Indians."

As he spoke there arose from the point of the horizon over the divide where the trail winds down into the plain a cloud of dust that hid from them for the moment the foe who was to cut athwart their hopes and plans. Then the figure of a horse and behind him of a man in a wagon, the figure of Queseo, were silhouetted against the western sky.

It was at this moment that Sayre leaning out of the window for a breath of the air which came sparingly that hot afternoon, saw far down the road, rising against the blue line of the horizon, another cloud of dust. In the perfect level of the plain it was long before he could discern clearly the object which he knew at once that this heralded, the daily stage which brought them their mail and their news from the outer world, and rare visitors, an inspector, perhaps, or an army officer, scarcely ever any other. For a time after Noseby's visit the mail had been looked forward to with apprehension. But the results feared had tarried now so long that in their work the thought of these had almost passed from the minds of the men always more occupied with hopes and plans than with fears.

As now along the dusty road the lumbering coach drew nearer and nearer, Sayre was far more interested in what Mr. Rathman, the missionary, was reading as to an opening promised his artist boy where he could work his way and still study than in any thought of his mail. He watched the coach absently, and as he caught sight of Queseo coming down the slope of the divide and about to reach the school,— if he were coming here,—at the same time with the stage, he smiled to himself through his listening at the thought of Queseo coming for the mail.

As the stage drew toward the door, the three on the bench rose and went to the piazza to be present at the event of the day, its arrival.

"Somebody's come," said Wasu in her own tongue, as she ran up the steps. "Perhaps it's company for Mrs. Sayre, and she'll want me."

Sayre had turned away again, and the people in the room were too busy to notice what was going on outside, until a scraggy hand worked at the fastenings of the stage door and a harsh voice called, "What 're you about? Let us out of this, can't you?"

At the same moment the door gave way and the speaker landed somewhat precipitately on the steps. He recovered himself, and turning, helped out two ladies, leaving the remaining occupant of the stage to follow them.

Sayre looked at the two men, one domineering, the other sly of face. He bent his head a moment, and his brows knitted. Then he rushed into the office where the mail was just being distributed.

The rest of the party collected from the parlor to the piazza. Here Mrs. Sayre's look of expectation was met by a stare from each member of the quartette.

"Won't you walk in?" she asked.

"I reckon we will," answered the older man with a laugh.

And pushing past, he attempted to lead the way.

But Mrs. Sayre was too quick for him; and it was she who held open the door of her parlor for the strangers. These filed in and seated themselves without even waiting for the invitation which was upon the lips of their hostess.

"I reckon you'd better take this lady to her room at once," pursued the elder of the two men; "or show her round an' she'll choose for herself. My wife an' I'll go up to the other house after a bit. Wouldn't you like to go with 'em, Eliza, an' wash your face an' freshen up for supper?"

Sayre coming into the room caught the last words. He exchanged a glance with his wife, and nodded to her without speaking.

"Wasu!" she called.

The girl came in. She looked at the two strange women with an insight which would have angered them could they have suspected anything under her staidness. For she could not have defined, but she saw that one was vinegar-faced and the other phlegmatic to stupidity.

"Show these ladies to the guest room, Wasu dear," said Mrs. Sayre.

"Is that the way you talk to Indians?" asked the younger woman with a toss of her head. "There's none of that trash about me, I can tell you." She cast a glance of defiance at Mrs.

Sayre and with her companion quitted the room in Wasu's wake.

Hutchins broke the seal of the letter which Sayre had just handed him, read and passed it back to him, receiving Sayre's own in exchange. "You are Mr. Barnes, the new agent?" he asked the older man. "And you are Mr. Green, the new superintendent?" he said to the other.

"Takes great acumen to discover us!" sneered he who was to be the schoolmaster. "Who else could we be, as you must have known days ago?"

"It's only in these letters just received that this information has come," returned Sayre; "or you'd have found us more ready for you."

"Not a doubt of it!" returned the new agent with his discordant laugh. "But, if I'm not mistaken, that's what the office wished to guard against, — you're being too ready for us, setting your Indians on their ear. Ready! I guess so."

" Sir !" thundered Sayre.

The man stopped, actually frightened by Sayre's look. " I — that's what was told me," he said.

" It's a lie, sir, *whoever* said it; and any more such information as you may have received you will keep to yourself, or say it out of my hearing. Remember that."

" I will," meekly returned the new agent.

As he turned his head, he caught sight of the face of an Indian looking in at the door, a wondering face, as if its owner could not take in the situation fully, and yet with dismay upon it, as if he had already perceived enough for dismay. Barnes had no wish to give himself away, as he put it. If Sayre would make no trouble, none should come through his indiscretion. He turned his back upon Wolf's Teeth with contempt, and began to speak to Hutchins.

It was Green who caught sight of an Indian face at the window, a face framed in lank hair and matted braids, its eyes glowing with a wild exultation, its lips shut tightly to repress the shout that seemed ready to break forth, its look turned now upon Barnes and then upon Sayre in a silent laughter that twisted every wrinkle into hideous contortion.

Fear seized upon Green. It seemed to him that a fiend was mocking at them. He turned deadly pale; he tried to withdraw his eyes from the window. But they were held there as if fascinated. And in another moment he found that the eyes in this face were looking at him, through him; they had found out his terror and were exulting in it, gloating over it. Then they turned to the new agent, and pierced to a disquiet there deeper than his arrogance.

They took in the dignity of Hutchins, the man whose words, as the Indians knew, were like his bullets which " hit every time."

They turned upon Sayre. Here was the keenest interest, the test of what the others were.

Sayre stood apart, silent, his eyes flashing, his brows knitted, his head thrown back. On one side his wife watched him ; on the other this Indian face.

Suddenly, he became conscious of scrutiny. He turned, — and met the flaming eyes of the Indian.

But these eyes in meeting his own, lost their fire, wavered, and fell.

The face disappeared from the window.

" Little white chief, he lost his scalp, as the white man say," muttered its owner. " But just the same his big heart beat. But this will not be for long. It our turn now."

"It's our turn now," he repeated
with all his exultation returned in the
knowledge that the power of Sayre and
Hutchins was gone, and that Sayre's
successor was afraid of Queseo, the
Indian chief. No animal was ever
quicker to note signs of terror in the
human animal born to dominate them
than were these Indian leaders who
longed for the savage life to note the
impression that they made upon these
specimens of the dominant white man
with whom they came in contact. It
takes civilization to respect an office in
spite of the man who fills it. The eye
of this new agent and that of the superintendent counted more to the Indians
than their seals of office.

It was what Queseo had found in the
eye of Green that sent him home with
the wild shout ringing out into the
night so soon as he had gone beyond
the reach of the agency settlement, for
he could not forget that Sayre and

Hutchins were still there. He had gone to the agency to ask a permission; he came back to announce a victory of which in spite of Noseby's insinuations and Pow-watz' faith he had not dared to dream.

In the summer twilight his waving arm could be seen as he drove up to the camps, and his cry of news brought the whole village about him.

"I'm chief again!" he cried. "And Pow-watz the medicine man. They 'kicked out'; that what the little white chief calls it. His big heart no use now. The new white men, they not have big heart; they afraid of Queseo, the Indian chief. Let them be. We keep them afraid."

Then his eye lighted upon Chekotoco who had followed his father to camp, and now stood among the returned students who had grouped themselves together as if to meet united the impending blow to their liberties.

For they knew how Hutchins and
Sayre had mitigated to them by every
possible means the evils of camp life.
The two men recognized in these young
people the solution of the Indian prob-
lem. And they saw in them also a
more personal appeal, a band of young
soldiers struggling to do their best in a
forlorn hope. They came to the res-
cue; they stimulated them to long for
and to try for the life of other young
Americans; they strove to put into
their hands the weapons of knowledge
and skill, and to bring up to their aid
the reserve forces of opportunity which
lagged so far in the rear.

All in a moment, this was over. But
even their despair did not recognize
how utterly until Queseo caught sight
of his son among them.

"Chekotoco!" called the chief in
tones that the young man then and
there did not think it wise to disregard.

He came forward.

"It not matter now if you twenty one," shrieked the chief. "Mr. Sayre not be here any longer to tell me you of age, you too old to obey your father. It not the white man's rule here now. You not forget that. Every young man will do as his father tell him. That's my orders."

His imitation of Sayre's tone and manner would have been amusing had not the situation been fatal for many of his listeners.

"We have a medicine dance now," announced Pow-watz.

The old rule had indeed come back; and no mourning for this dared show itself in face of the blatant exultation. All the summer night the chief, the medicine man, and a few other choice spirits with them sat in conference, and in their plotting to grasp the reins of power over their people firmly once more, not one Indian who was doing his best to become civilized was forgotten.

The young men were portioned out to one and another to be brought into subjection.

With the disappearance of the face from the window Green breathed freely again, and began to question Mrs. Sayre in regard to the building, the rooms and the pupils. He did not quite like to speak to Sayre, that silence of his was too formidable

As they were talking, the two women returned. Mrs. Sayre explained to Mrs. Green that their ignorance of the change of superintendents had made it impossible to be ready for them, but that in a few days they would be ready to leave the field in order to the new comers.

"In a few days!" shrieked Mrs. Green. "What am *I* to do in the mean time? I can't do anything with other people round. Our position dates from today noon. You'll have to be packed and out of this tonight."

Sayre looked up sharply. He was about to speak, then checked himself and stood silent with head erect. They had many friends among the Indians. If there should come to these an idea of any dissension, and such an idea would fly quickly, there would be trouble, annoyance and bitterness if nothing more serious. This should not be.

" My last month's salary has not come yet through some detention," he said finally with studied quietness. " My home is hundreds of miles off, and I shall be obliged to ask your forbearance for a day until I can get at some money; for,—not looking for this,—I'm short."

"Why," began Mrs. Rathman, "you must come"— when she stopped in wonder at a figure that strode into the room. Wasu had returned and was standing beside Mrs. Sayre. It was Wolf's Teeth who came in with a glance far from friendly at the new comers, and walked directly up to Sayre.

"Mr. Sayre," he began, "I have house. My squaw and me, we go outside; you and Mrs. Sayre, you come in there. I not forget when you give me your best room. I give you mine. You not stay where they not want you. Indians give you all they have; they proud to have you in their houses."

Mrs. Sayre's head went down with a sob on Wasu's shoulder.

Sayre choked. "Thank you, Wolf's Teeth," he said brokenly, and grasped the dark hand held out to him.

"You want money," pursued Wolf's Teeth. "I got it here in my pocket,— thirty dollars. And I go round to the Indians, I get you five hundred quicker 'n you can talk. You say so, they give it to you. They like the white man's way,—some white man's way," he added with a sweeping glance of scorn at the new officials. "You take this now; I get you more." And he thrust a roll of bills into Sayre's hand. "I earn it all myself," he added; "you keep that if you want it."

"Thank you, my kind friend," said the little, dark man, his eyes glistening. "I will borrow this of you while I need it. But do not get me any more." Not for worlds would he thrust back the money upon the Indian then and there. But he would return him his own bills again before he left the reservation.

"This won't do, Catherine," said Green in an undertone to his wife. "See here, Mrs. Sayre," he added aloud, "of course you'll stay here as long as you need to; we sha'n't think of anything else. Do you want the Indians glowering at us?" he asked in another aside. "You'd better take care."

To go to Mrs. Rathman's with their family, although urgently invited, would have seriously inconvenienced the missionaries. To accept Wolf's Teeth's offer, to say nothing of its inconvenience, would publish disagreement with the new . people, — although for the moment Sayre was tempted to do it. Under the circumstances they had a right to remain at the school.

And they did so.

The following evening Hutchins and Sayre with their families quitted the reservation.

Their hearts were heavy as they realized the troubles that must come from the men who had taken their places, and feared the despair and wreck that would come to many lives under the old Indian rule which Sayre had seen in his glance at Quesco's face was purposed, even if the next day had not brought assurance of this.

For Pow-watz had come to demand rather than to ask a medicine dance; and his lowering visage had secured to him all his desires. It had been one of the triumphs not to be soon forgotten that this demand had been granted to him in the very face of Hutchins whose beginning of explanation of the danger of it had been met by the statement that he was "out" now, and that it belonged to those who were "in" to decide such matters.

Hereafter Pow-watz would have a clearer idea than ever of what being "out" meant.

VII

MRS. SAYRE had tried so hard to bring Wasu away with her. It would also have been the surest way to get hold of Chekotoco.

Wolf's Teeth would have been glad; but her mother refused. The agent also had interfered. Wasu was the best trained girl in housework in the school; Mrs. Green needed her help. It was meddlesome in them to have any longer interest in the Indians, and, turned out with ignominy as they had been, they had better leave things alone.

They had tried to have Wasu married at Mr. Rathmam's that evening of their deposition. But Chekotoco, not foreseeing any such arrangement, had fol-

lowed his father to camp, and had not
returned the next day, being in fact
kept prisoner by Queseo who chose
that he should have no final talk with
Sayre. Mr. Rathman, however, promised to look after the two, to marry
them, and, if possible, to send them out
of the reservation to the place that
Sayre had opened for them.

Sayre wrote Chekotoco all final direc-
tions, wrote his friend that Hutchins
and himself had been kicked out of the
service as if they had disgraced it, but
that the young Indian with his wife
would probably be with him at about
such a time.

Then he waited for news of them.

The letter to Chekotoco reached the
office. Barnes had taken upon himself
the duty of distributing the mail. He
and Green decided that the letter was
from Sayre, and that it was not for
their interest to deliver it. They
pigeon-holed it. In case of necessity

it could appear as something over-looked.

At the time of its arrival the young man was hanging about the school, waiting to see Wasu. It was only two days from the time set for their wedding, and they perceived not the smallest preparation. Mr. Rathman who realized that being upon bad terms with the new people would hamper his work, had taken no action in the matter further than gaining a promise from Wasu that she would come to him if she needed him.

" Have you asked her?" said the young man as he and Wasu stood talking together.

Wasu answered her lover that she had not. " She so cross," added the girl. " She say she need me all the time, I too big to go to school any longer, I know enough. Mrs. Sayre, she always told me to study more, it do me good. I do what Mrs. Sayre tells me. I go to school every afternoon. I get out of her way, too," said the Indian girl with a shrewd smile. "You ask Mr. Green, Chekotoco," she went on.

"I did ask him. He said he was too busy to talk about it. You ask her tomorrow."

"Yes, I will," returned Wasu.

And then Mrs. Green called her.

"Don't be standing round talking to young men, Wasu; it's very bad in you," she said sharply as the girl entered the house.

Wasu's eyes opened wide; she turned breathless a moment in amazement and anger. Then she began,

"Chekotoco"—

"I don't want to hear one word about Chekotoco," interrupted the other. "Put your thoughts upon your work and see if you can't wash those dishes quicker than you did yesterday. My gracious! such slowness! I can't stand it."

It was true that Wasu was slow; but she was very thorough, and she was conscientious to a remarkable degree. When Mrs. Sayre had wanted to hurry her she used to run a race with her and would sometimes let the girl come out ahead laughing at her triumph. Then she would say, "Wasu, you got up steam that time." It had been so easy to work then Wasu said to herself that afternoon, and even things she did not like to do had always gone off well when Mrs. Sayre was round. She did not go off to her work in response to Mrs. Green's order. She faced the wife of the new superintendent.

"Chekotoco and I be married the day after tomorrow," she announced. "Mrs. Sayre, she was going to give us a wedding, and have lemonade for the Indians; we have a fine time. Didn't she tell you about it?"

"A wedding! And lemonade! And all the Indians howling around here?

Goodness gracious! 'Twould drive me wild to think of it. What a crazy notion. None of such nonsense for me."

Wasu did not know what " crazy" meant; but she did understand and resent the word " nonsense." Her temper which under Mrs. Sayre's judicious and affectionate treatment had seemed to have no existence, began to flame. But she still controlled herself.

" Didn't Mrs. Sayre tell you ? " she repeated.

" No, indeed ! " returned the other.

A shadow fell over Wasu's face. " I be married the day after tomorrow just the same," she said. " I promise Chekotoco."

" What of that ? Tell him you've changed your mind. Lots of white girls do that. I promised three men and changed my mind before I married Mr. Green."

" I should think he not have you,"

returned Wasu. "He better not," she added.

The other's face crimsoned with fury. She stamped her foot. But something in the Indian girl's look restrained her. As soon as she could command her voice, she said.

"Just for your impertinence, if nothing else, I sha'n't let you be married till I'm ready. I've got to train somebody to take your place first, and I sha'n't hurry, I tell you."

"I not know what impertinence means," answered Wasu. "But I promised Chekotoco, and I marry him."

"Don't answer me back again, and go to your work. You will do as I tell you. That's what we're here for, to make the Indians mind."

Nevertheless, she was slightly astonished when the girl disappeared.

Ten minutes later she went into the kitchen to find it empty.

Wasu had run over to the missionary's with all her speed.

She told her story with the pathos of helplessness mingling with her anger. "Mrs. Sayre promise me she tell her about the wedding," she said with a grief over betrayed friendship deeper than her anger.

"Mrs. Sayre did tell her, Wasu," cried Mrs. Rathman, "I heard her myself."

"And Mrs. Green, she tell me a lie?" cried the girl. "I never go into her house again ; she not fit for Indians."

Mr. Rathman's moustache concealed his smile, and Mrs. Rathman looked at her with shining eyes.

"But what will you do, Wasu dear?" she asked.

"I stay with you."

"I should be too glad to have you ; but it would make trouble with those people. Still, you shall not be sent away."

"I not make trouble," returned Wasu. "I go home." But the tone was sad. For Wasu's mother was a camp Indian; she often wandered off from Wolf's Teeth to the freedom of the Indian village, and if she had control of Wasu, there was little doubt but that she would take the girl with her whether Wasu wished it or not. The young girl perceived all this, for tears ran over her downcast face. "There's plenty of room in the camps," she added, "they always like Indians in the camps."

And then she began to sob.

"No, no, dear child, you shall not go there," cried the missionary's wife. "I have it, Will," she said to her husband. "Marry them on the spot. Send for Chekotoco this moment."

"I'll do it!" cried Rathman. And he sent his messenger.

"Chekotoco must be right round here," said Wasu drying her eyes.

Mrs. Rathman brought out some cake,

made coffee in place of the coveted
lemonade, and found a ring that would
serve as a wedding ring, for she comprehended that the need of symbols is
in inverse ratio to the presence of civilization. She sent for Wolf's Teeth, and
when he came she explained the circumstances to him as well as she could
without saying evil of Mrs. Green and
speaking too plainly of the situation
generally.

But the Indian saw as clearly as she
did. He approved of the step.

"They hold on to the young Indians down in the camp," he said.
"They not let them marry white man's
way. I not want Wasu there. She
marry Chekotoco now; and then she go
back to the school. And Mr. Sayre, he
send soon, he always do as he say.
Then they go way off. It hard for
me; but it better for them. I do like
the white man."

At the end of the simple service Mrs.

Green and her husband and the agent
walked in. The woman was white with
rage, and treated the company to a few
expressions more forcible than elegant.
She flatly refused to take back Wasu;
she attacked the missionaries for abet-
ting the girl in disobedience, and declared that the camp was the best place
for such Indians.

Chekotoco raised his head haughtily.

"We go to camp," he said. "My
father Indian chief. We stay there till
Mr. Sayre send for us. Come, Wasu."

The girl's tears came again.

"No, you shall not go to camp, you
shall stay here with us," cried Mrs.
Rathman. "You shall work in the
mission till you go away."

Mr. Rathman seconded the invitation
heartily.

The girl looked up at her young
husband wistfully.

"Fine encouragement to insubordination you're setting," cried Mr. Barnes.

"I declare, you shall be reported as mischief makers, interfering between us and our duties. You shall suffer for this."

Chekotoco's decision was made.

"They shall not suffer for us, Wasu," he said. "They've been kind to us. We thank you." And he turned to the missionaries. "Come, Wasu," he said again. "Mr. Sayre send soon."

Barnes and Green exchanged glances. They believed that Mr. Sayre's letter was where it would take some time in reaching the young people.

"No, we not do that," said Wasu sadly. And Wolf's Teeth joined them. "We live all right in the camp, Mrs. Rathman," said the young bride. "We make other Indians want to come and get married, too."

And so, in spite of all persuasions, they went away.

Barnes never troubled himself to learn what followed.

But three weeks later he received a letter from Sayre's friend who, having heard no word from the young Indians, wrote to inquire about them. Barnes returned answer that they had gone back to camp like all Indians, and were probably as bad as the worst; it often happened so.

The inquirer was convinced that his friend Sayre was too big-hearted to be anything but a "crank" on Indian matters, and Sayre could never get a satisfactory explanation of the reason why the other had changed his mind and would take no more trouble in the matter, in spite of the urgency of the ex-superintendent when he learned the whole story.

Three days had gone by, three days never to be forgotten in the lives of these two young Indians who had found among their own people the iron hand of a despotism that the civilized world has outgrown. Quesco would by no means endure that his own son should defy his rule,—this would be an exception which would make everthing incomplete.

As to a girl, she was scarcely worth the thought necessary to bring her into submission. Poor Wasu was hoping that she would be considered of too little consequence to be remembered at all on this day which was so full of importance to the wild Indians, the day of the great dance. She had said to herself that if she could not stay at the camps and live a civilized life, it would be easy to go back again to Mrs. Rathman.

But it was not so. Chekotoco was to be made an example of submission, and she, as the wife of the chief's son, was to be fitted for him in all Indian ways.

She hid her face in her hands as she recalled with a shudder the looks and words of the squaws who had told her this in more forceful terms than words alone, as they had torn off from her roughly the clothing she had worn to camp and had put the Indian dress in its place.

And when she had put on another one from her trunk which Mrs. Green had sent after her, this had been treated in the same way, and the trunk taken from her. She must wear the Indian dress, or nothing.

But the dance was about to begin. If they would only forget her! And where was Chekotoco? She had not seen him all day, not since he had left the tepee when Pow-watz had sent for him that morning.

Why would not this be a good time to run away to the agency, to run away from the reservation altogether? They were like white people, and these would help them.

And then Wasu remembered her Indian dress; and again she buried in her hands the face that she had lifted in a momentary hope, and sobbed bitterly.

Oh, where was Mr. Sayre's letter? Where was Mrs. Sayre's love for her? Why had she and Chekotoco known better at all, if this was to be the end of it? What did they go to school and learn white ways for, if it was only to have more pain?

Poor little Wasu! Here she was in the forefront of the battle, helpless, as unarmed as ignorance, overawed by the tyranny to which her early training had made her susceptible, and, more even than this, she had been under physical compulsion and might be again at any moment.

Chekotoco and she were indeed in the forefront of the battle, and all the forces which should have brought aid had retired and left them unsupported.

As Wasu sobbed on, softly, lest even this noise should betray her, her quick ear caught the sound of steps.

She listened.

They were coming nearer.

She threw her glance about the tepee; and with the step of a cat crept to a pile of robes thrown upon the floor, and in the stifling heat opened the mass and plunged into it, throwing the robes entirely over herself as she crouched on the earth, leaving only a little space close by the ground for breath.

The steps came to the door of the tepee, and stopped.

Three squaws, one of them Cheko-toco's mother, looked in.

"She run away," said one.

"No," said the chief's squaw; "I watch the tepee all day; and Wa-sa-jah watch other side. Queseo say so. She's here, Who-lac-cy."

The search began.

"I told you she's here," said the leader, dragging out Wasu.

They led her off in triumph. They

prepared her for the dance. Two held her hands, and the third painted her face. She found that struggle was only likely to get the paint into her eyes and mouth, and so she stood still. Then they unbound her hair.

At the end of their labors it would have been impossible to recognize Wasu, the school girl. She was completely an Indian squaw. Only He that looketh not on the outward appearance could know that she was just the same with only an added hate of Indian ways.

It was her mother who led her out into the space where the dancers were assembled.

Wolf's Teeth was not there.

Here were the squaws hideous with paint, and the braves even more hideous. The tomtoms were beating, the men and women were taking their places. Eyes always hard were growing harder with the glint of excitement in them.

Pow-watz at Queseo's elbow presided and governed all things. His cruel eyes took in the shrinking Wasu, and watched as Chekotoco in the full Indian rig which had been forced upon him by threats that Wasu should never hear, threats of danger to her, crossed the space and came up to her.

Others were watching, also, young people like these, who, like these, had submitted to their hard fate, whose eyes were full of pity for the two, and for one another, but whose lips dared utter here no word of sympathy.

But Wasu and Chekotoco in that moment saw only each other.

She put her hand into his, and he held it firmly.

"We have to do it," he whispered to her. We are Indians, and only Indians. All the rest has gone far away. This is all that is left. This is our home. We must live in our home."

He led her into the dance where

Queseo and Pow-watz had commanded their attendance.

And in so doing he led her into the old Indian life.

What bitter tears, what sorrows are before them!

And like them there are hundreds, — yes, thousands.